When I Grow UP

Kathy Gueye

To order additional copies of this book, contact:
Xlibris
1-888-795-4274
www.Xlibris.com
Orders@Xlibris.com

When I Grow UP

Kathy Gueye

Acknowledgements

With gratitude and thanks, I wish to acknowledge every person the universe has placed in my path to illuminate my existence and inspire me to write this book. I would like to especially thank Antoneal Griffiths, for bringing my vision alive through his illustrations.

I would like to thank in memory my mother Hazel Cuffy Wheeler and my father David Wheeler, my daughter Asiba, my son Keba-Tarik, my grandchildren Aniya, J'adore, Ayden, (granddaughter on her way into this planet), brother Steven, neices Naimah and Dion, nephews Jamaal, and Malik, Sisters Denise, in memory Marlene and Michelle and a host of other family and friends.

I would like to acknowledge a few but not in the very least all, the people who believed in this journey and encouraged me along the way with your love and support , Tracey Lissimore, Jennifer Fields, Fatima Curry-Jenkins, Sabrina Battles, Robyn Ford, Roxanne Woodard, Keisha Baxter, Syeatta Bolden, Antoine Jackson, Fame Productions, for his great mind and photographs, NYCHollywood for your support and energy! Last but not least all of the staff who helped to make this book a reality, with their hard work Xlibris Publishing.

I am grateful for the opportunity to live in a country where anyone can be The President!

Dedication

I dedicate this book to all of the children I have spent time with, worked with, played with, read to, for the inspiration to write a book which celebrates imagination which allows thoughts to become reality.

It is because of your gift to the world and the divine spirit, the foundation is set through imagination and play, opening doors for exploration in the world.

One bright sunny day
Tarik was not feeling well.
No outside play today
instead he had to stay in bed.
He was sad because his friends
were outside playing their favorite
game Let's Pretend. Tarik said, "Boy,
it is going to be a long day".

Jamaal played with his paper airplane
Flying it high
Up in the clouds
Up in the sky . . .

Malik pretended to fly like the birds
Looking down to see far away lands
Over vast oceans, rivers, and seas
He said " I know what I want to be
When I grow up!"

Aniya sat on the beach
up high on the lifeguard bench.
She could see the ocean waves
beat against the shore.
Aniya said, "When I grow up Im going to
swim so I can save people who need help".

Ayden played with his truck, "Vroom, Vroom!"
He loved to pretend he drove to far away places
Where he saw different races, and faces.
"I want to drive trucks when I grow up", Ayden said.

Mom and Dad said, today
is very important because
history will be made!

All the grown ups
Were gathered around
Watching the television
Listening to the news
Something great was
Happening!

Later that evening
Tarik sat up in bed,
when he heard laughter, clapping, cheers.
"Yeah! Hooray! Amazing!"
Grandpa said, "never thought this would
Happen in my day! I don't know what to say"
Everyone was so happy to see
Our new President Barack Obama
A man who looked like me!!!

Tarik said, "When I grow up I
want to be President!"

Antoneal Griffiths was born in Jamaica, West Indies. His passion for art, began in childhood continuing to this day. Throughout his life, he was greatly influenced by his father Carl Griffiths who was an avid photographer. Antoneal Griffiths spent most of his childhood and currently resides in New Jersey. He attended West Side High School and East Orange High School where he perfected his craft, expanding his knowledge through various artistic genres.

CPSIA information can be obtained at www.ICGtesting.com
Printed in the USA
BVIW12n1305070918
526755BV00004B/8